Disney KINGDOMS

# BIG THUNDER MOUNTAIN RAILROAD

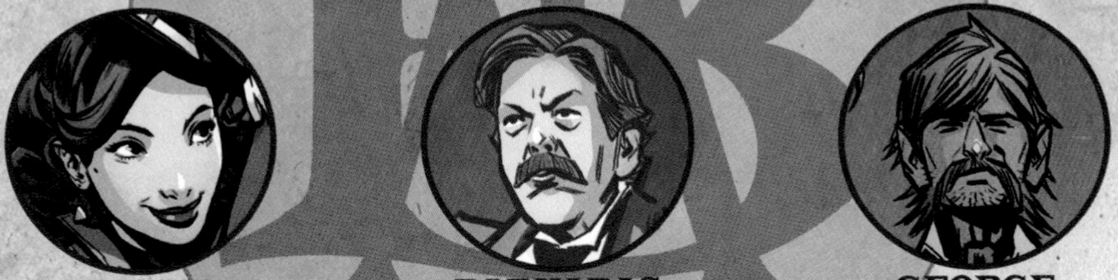

ABIGAIL BULLION — BARNABAS T. BULLION — GEORGE WILLIKERS

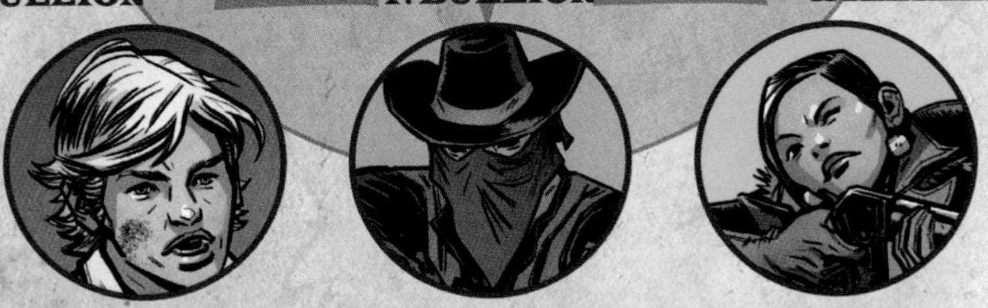

CHANDLER — DOLFO — ONAWA

## BIG THUNDER MOUNTAIN RAILROAD #4

**ABIGAIL BULLION** just arrived in Rainbow Ridge, the western town built around the Big Thunder Mountain gold mine owned by her father, **BARNABAS T. BULLION.**

Abby came to Big Thunder at a tough time—business hasn't been great, and her father is forcing the miners to dig deeper and deeper. Many of the men, including **CHANDLER**, warn that the increase in accidents is a result of the anger of the spirit of Big Thunder.

It turns out that Chandler, along with fellow Rainbow Ridge residents **ONAWA** and **DOLFO**, are members of a crew of bandits who steal from the mine, recently taking off with a whole train's worth of gold. When Abby, out of loyalty to her father, tried to stop them, she found out that the bandits use the gold for much-needed supplies to help the town survive. To make matters worse, she discovers that her father and his foreman, **WILLIKERS**, risked miners' lives by forcing them to stay underground during a dangerous flash flood!

Horrified, Abby decided there was only one thing to do: become a bandit herself!


**DENNIS HOPELESS** writer

**TIGH WALKER with GUILLERMO MOGORRON** artists

**JEAN-FRANCOIS BEAULIEU** colorist

**VC's JOE CARAMAGNA** letterer

**MARCIO TAKARA and ESTHER SANZ** cover artists

**BRIAN CROSBY** connecting variant cover artist

**BRIAN CROSBY, ANDY DIGENOVA, TOM MORRIS & JOSH SHIPLEY** walt disney imagineers

**EMILY SHAW and MARK BASSO** editors

**AXEL ALONSO** editor in chief

**JOE QUESADA** chief creative officer

**DAN BUCKLEY** publisher



special thanks to
**BILL ROSEMANN, DAVID GABRIEL & MARK PANICCIA**

MARVEL

ABDO Spotlight

## ABDOPUBLISHING.COM

Reinforced library bound edition published in 2017 by Spotlight,
a division of ABDO, PO Box 398166, Minneapolis, Minnesota 55439.
Spotlight produces high-quality reinforced library bound editions for
schools and libraries. Published by agreement with Marvel Characters, Inc.

Printed in the United States of America, North Mankato, Minnesota.
092016
012017

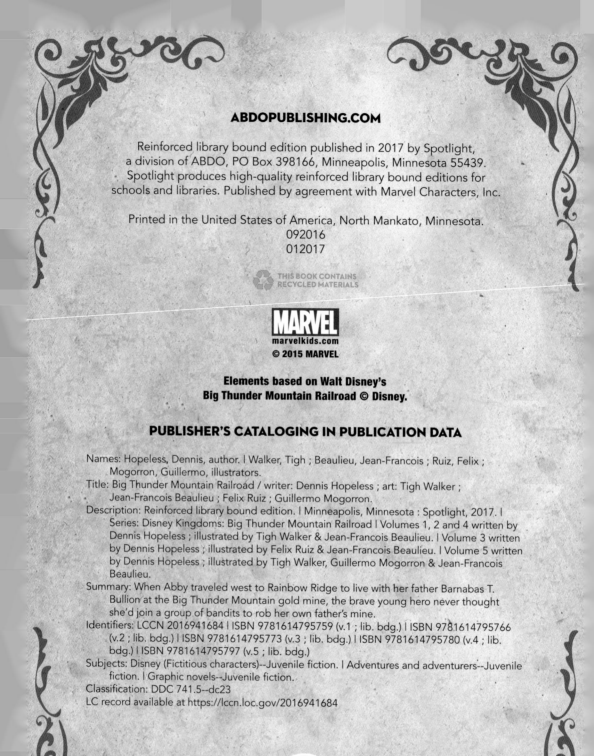

**MARVEL**
marvelkids.com

Elements based on Walt Disney's
Big Thunder Mountain Railroad © Disney.

## PUBLISHER'S CATALOGING IN PUBLICATION DATA

Names: Hopeless, Dennis, author. | Walker, Tigh ; Beaulieu, Jean-Francois ; Ruiz, Felix ;
  Mogorron, Guillermo, illustrators.
Title: Big Thunder Mountain Railroad / writer: Dennis Hopeless ; art: Tigh Walker ;
  Jean-Francois Beaulieu ; Felix Ruiz ; Guillermo Mogorron.
Description: Reinforced library bound edition. | Minneapolis, Minnesota : Spotlight, 2017. |
  Series: Disney Kingdoms: Big Thunder Mountain Railroad | Volumes 1, 2 and 4 written by
  Dennis Hopeless ; illustrated by Tigh Walker & Jean-Francois Beaulieu. | Volume 3 written
  by Dennis Hopeless ; illustrated by Felix Ruiz & Jean-Francois Beaulieu. | Volume 5 written
  by Dennis Hopeless ; illustrated by Tigh Walker, Guillermo Mogorron & Jean-Francois
  Beaulieu.
Summary: When Abby traveled west to Rainbow Ridge to live with her father Barnabas T.
  Bullion at the Big Thunder Mountain gold mine, the brave young hero never thought
  she'd join a group of bandits to rob her own father's mine.
Identifiers: LCCN 2016941684 | ISBN 9781614795759 (v.1 ; lib. bdg.) | ISBN 9781614795766
  (v.2 ; lib. bdg.) | ISBN 9781614795773 (v.3 ; lib. bdg.) | ISBN 9781614795780 (v.4 ; lib.
  bdg.) | ISBN 9781614795797 (v.5 ; lib. bdg.)
Subjects: Disney (Fictitious characters)--Juvenile fiction. | Adventures and adventurers--Juvenile
  fiction. | Graphic novels--Juvenile fiction.
Classification: DDC 741.5--dc23
LC record available at https://lccn.loc.gov/2016941684

**ABDO**

Spotlight

A Division of ABDO
abdopublishing.com

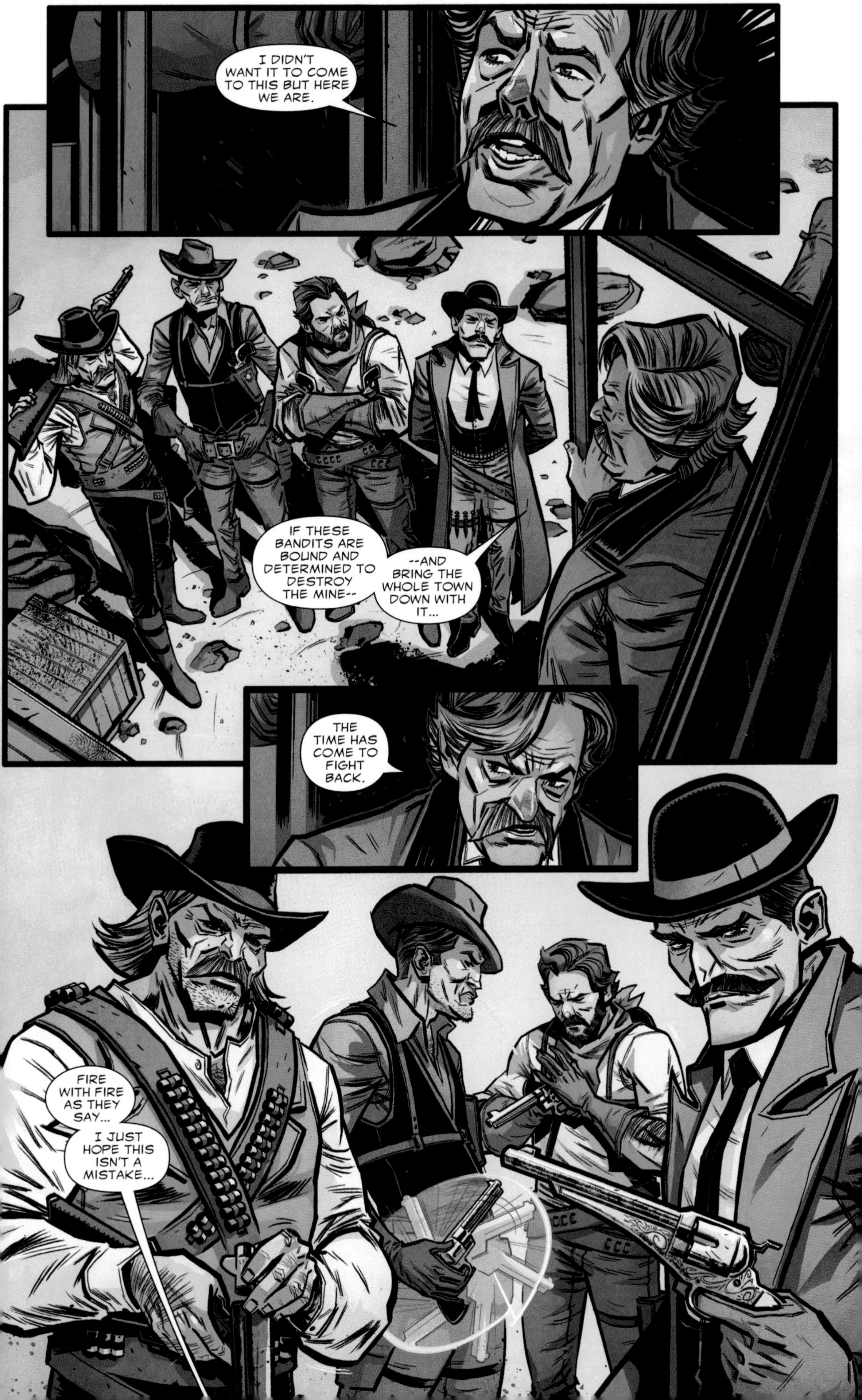
I DIDN'T WANT IT TO COME TO THIS BUT HERE WE ARE.
IF THESE BANDITS ARE BOUND AND DETERMINED TO DESTROY THE MINE--
--AND BRING THE WHOLE TOWN DOWN WITH IT...
THE TIME HAS COME TO FIGHT BACK.
FIRE WITH FIRE AS THEY SAY...
I JUST HOPE THIS ISN'T A MISTAKE...

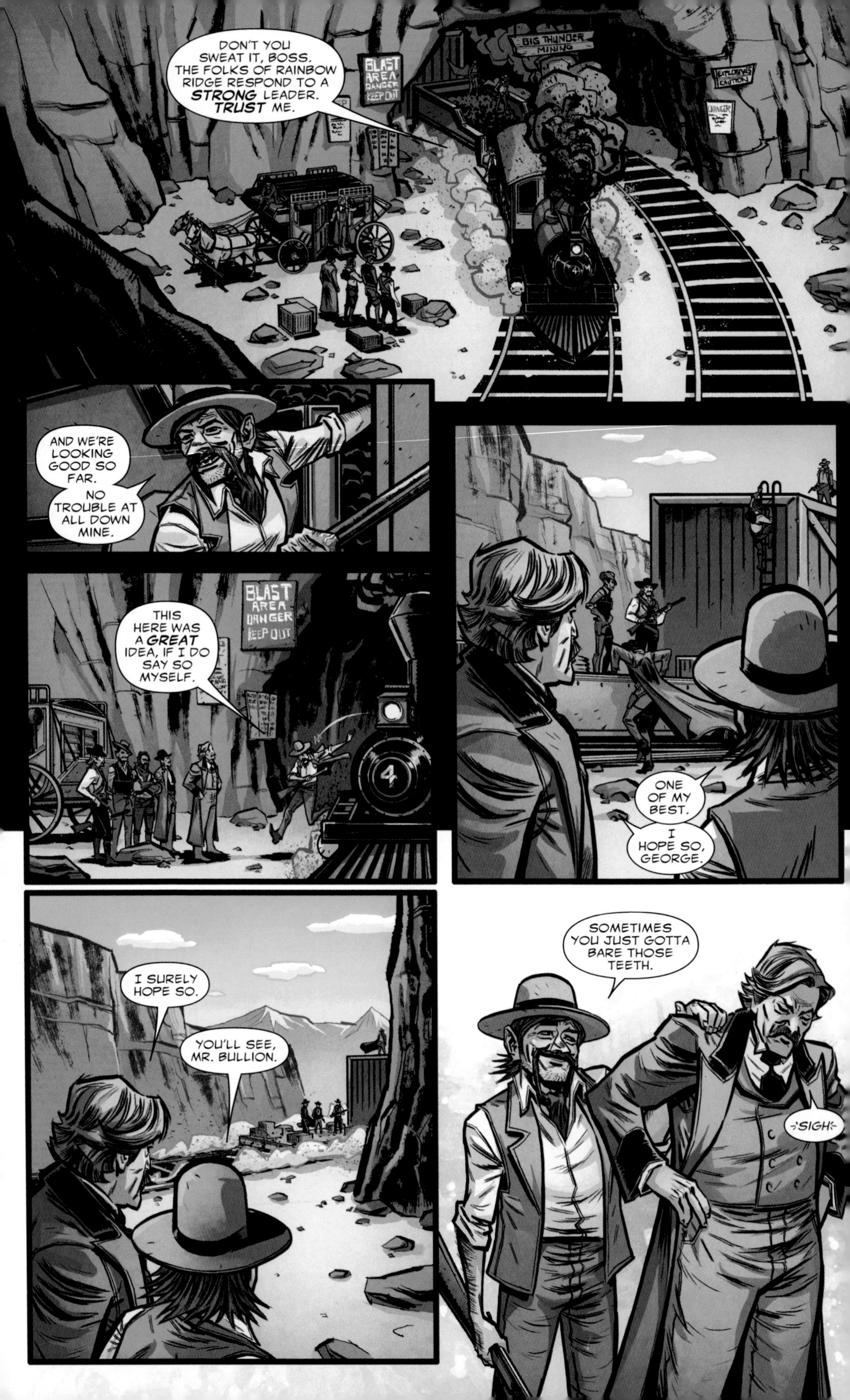

BIG THUNDER MINING
BLAST AREA DANGER KEEP OUT
EXPLOSIVES CAUTION
DANGER
DON'T YOU SWEAT IT, BOSS. THE FOLKS OF RAINBOW RIDGE RESPOND TO A STRONG LEADER. TRUST ME.
AND WE'RE LOOKING GOOD SO FAR.
NO TROUBLE AT ALL DOWN MINE.
BLAST AREA DANGER KEEP OUT
THIS HERE WAS A GREAT IDEA, IF I DO SAY SO MYSELF.
4
ONE OF MY BEST.
I HOPE SO, GEORGE.
I SURELY HOPE SO.
YOU'LL SEE, MR. BULLION.
SOMETIMES YOU JUST GOTTA BARE THOSE TEETH.
SIGH

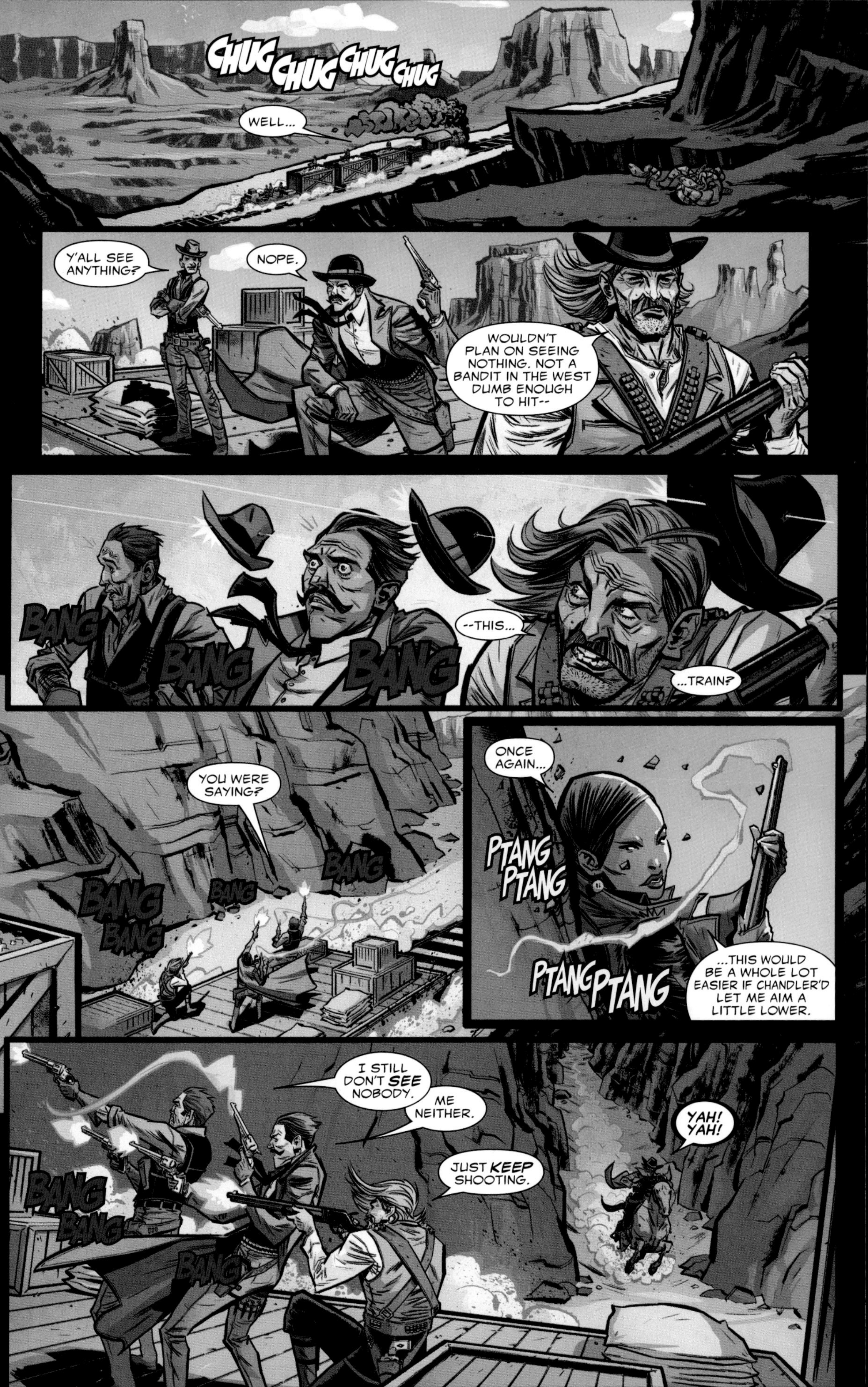

CHUG CHUG CHUG CHUG
WELL...
Y'ALL SEE ANYTHING?
NOPE.
WOULDN'T PLAN ON SEEING NOTHING. NOT A BANDIT IN THE WEST DUMB ENOUGH TO HIT--
BANG
BANG
BANG
--THIS...
...TRAIN?
YOU WERE SAYING?
BANG
BANG
BANG
BANG
ONCE AGAIN...
PTANG
PTANG
PTANG PTANG
...THIS WOULD BE A WHOLE LOT EASIER IF CHANDLER'D LET ME AIM A LITTLE LOWER.
I STILL DON'T SEE NOBODY.
ME NEITHER.
JUST KEEP SHOOTING.
YAH! YAH!
BANG
BANG
BANG

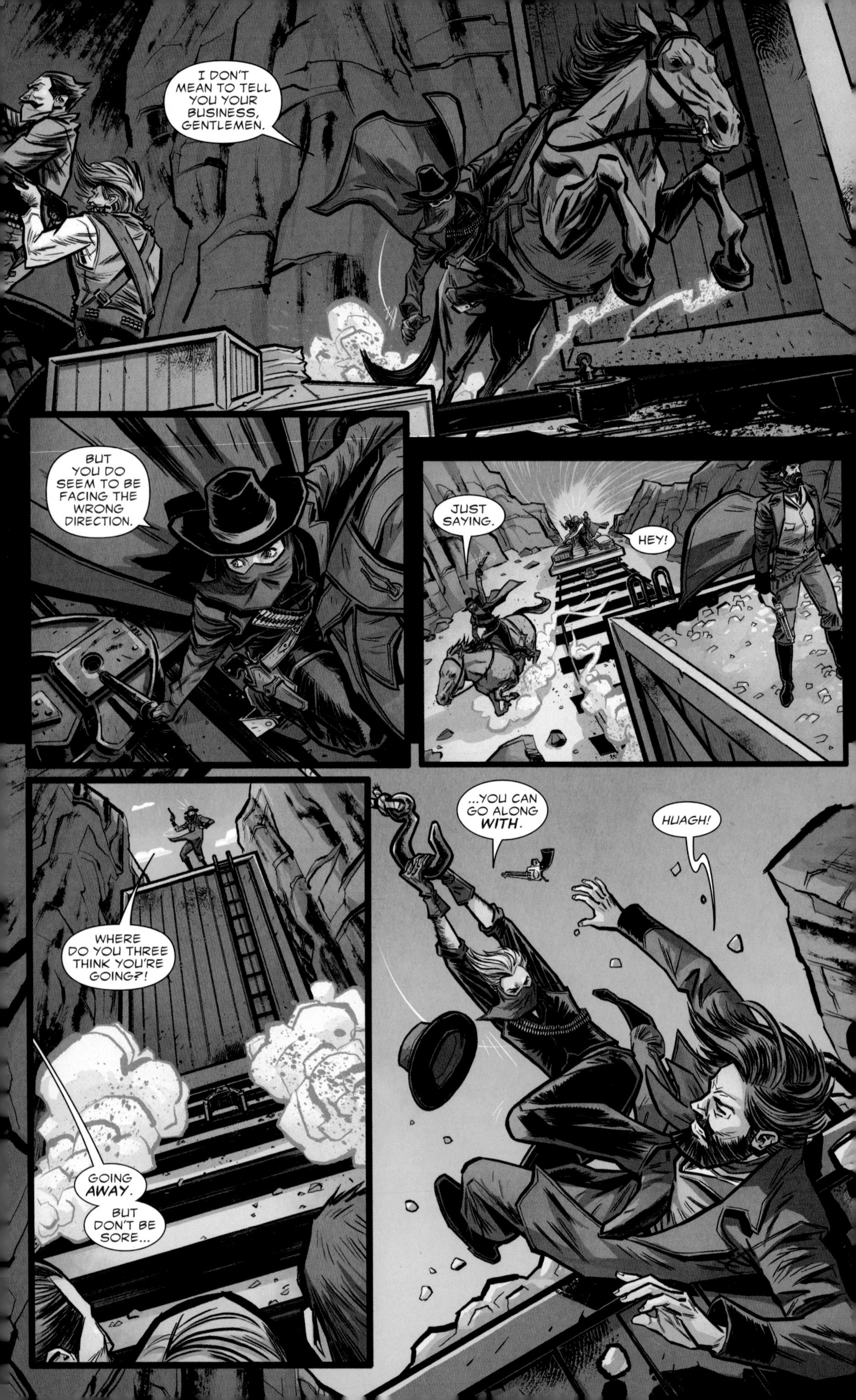
I DON'T MEAN TO TELL YOU YOUR BUSINESS, GENTLEMEN.
BUT YOU DO SEEM TO BE FACING THE WRONG DIRECTION.
JUST SAYING.
HEY!
WHERE DO YOU THREE THINK YOU'RE GOING?!
GOING *AWAY*.
BUT DON'T BE SORE...
...YOU CAN GO ALONG *WITH*.
HUAGH!

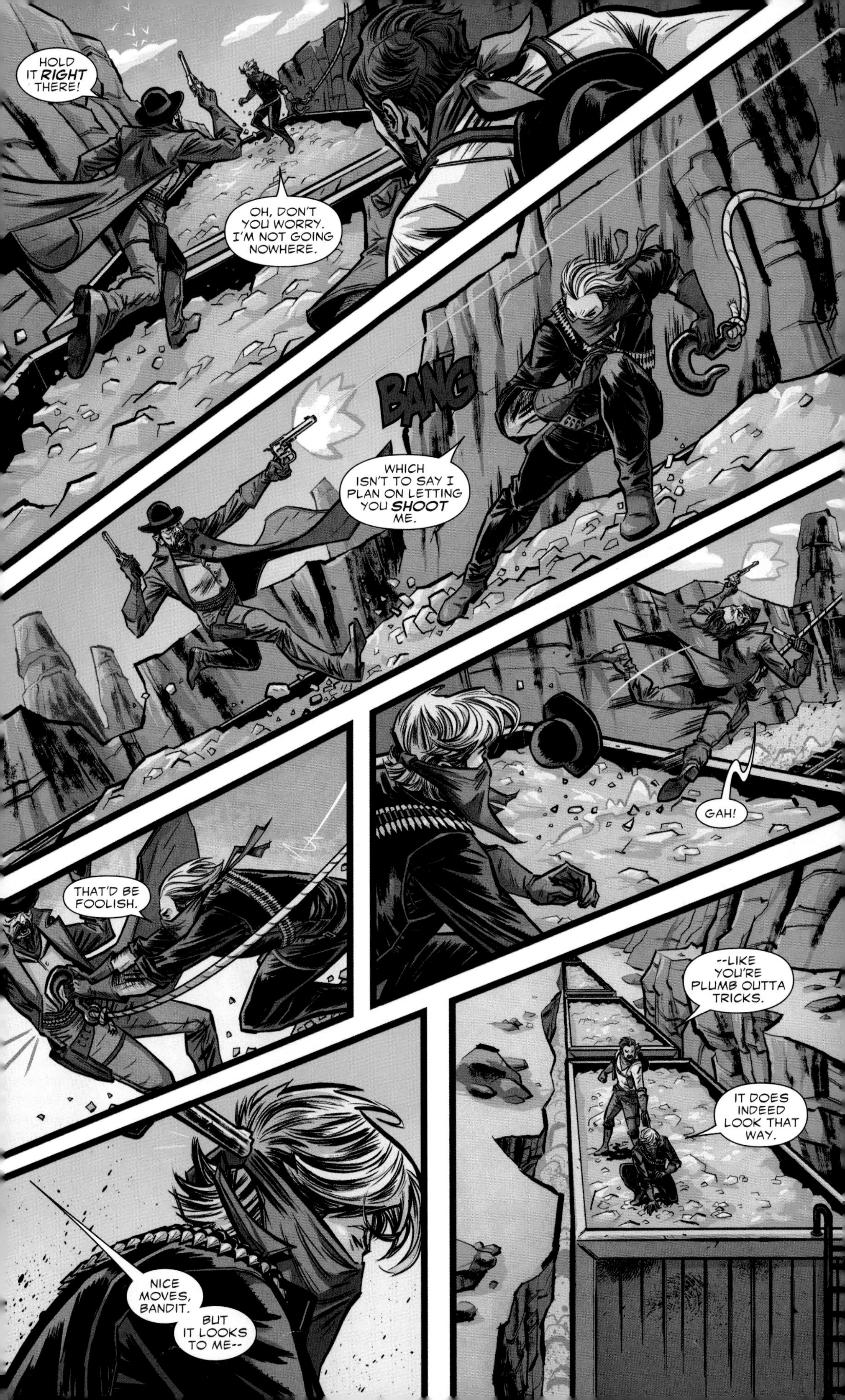
HOLD IT RIGHT THERE!
OH, DON'T YOU WORRY. I'M NOT GOING NOWHERE.
BANG
WHICH ISN'T TO SAY I PLAN ON LETTING YOU SHOOT ME.
GAH!
THAT'D BE FOOLISH.
NICE MOVES, BANDIT.
BUT IT LOOKS TO ME--
--LIKE YOU'RE PLUMB OUTTA TRICKS.
IT DOES INDEED LOOK THAT WAY.

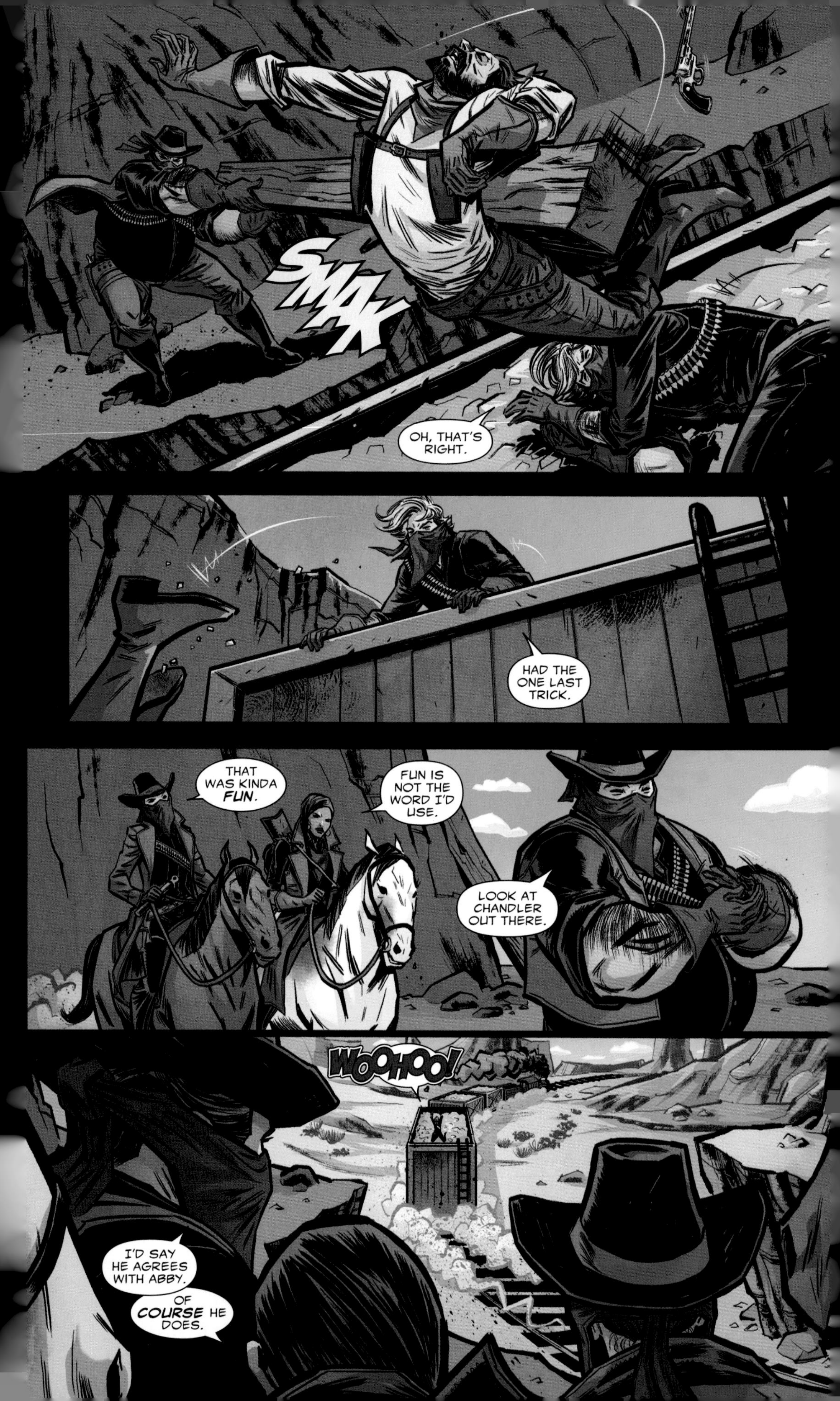
SMAK
OH, THAT'S RIGHT.
HAD THE ONE LAST TRICK.
THAT WAS KINDA FUN.
FUN IS NOT THE WORD I'D USE.
LOOK AT CHANDLER OUT THERE.
WOOHOO!
I'D SAY HE AGREES WITH ABBY.
OF COURSE HE DOES.

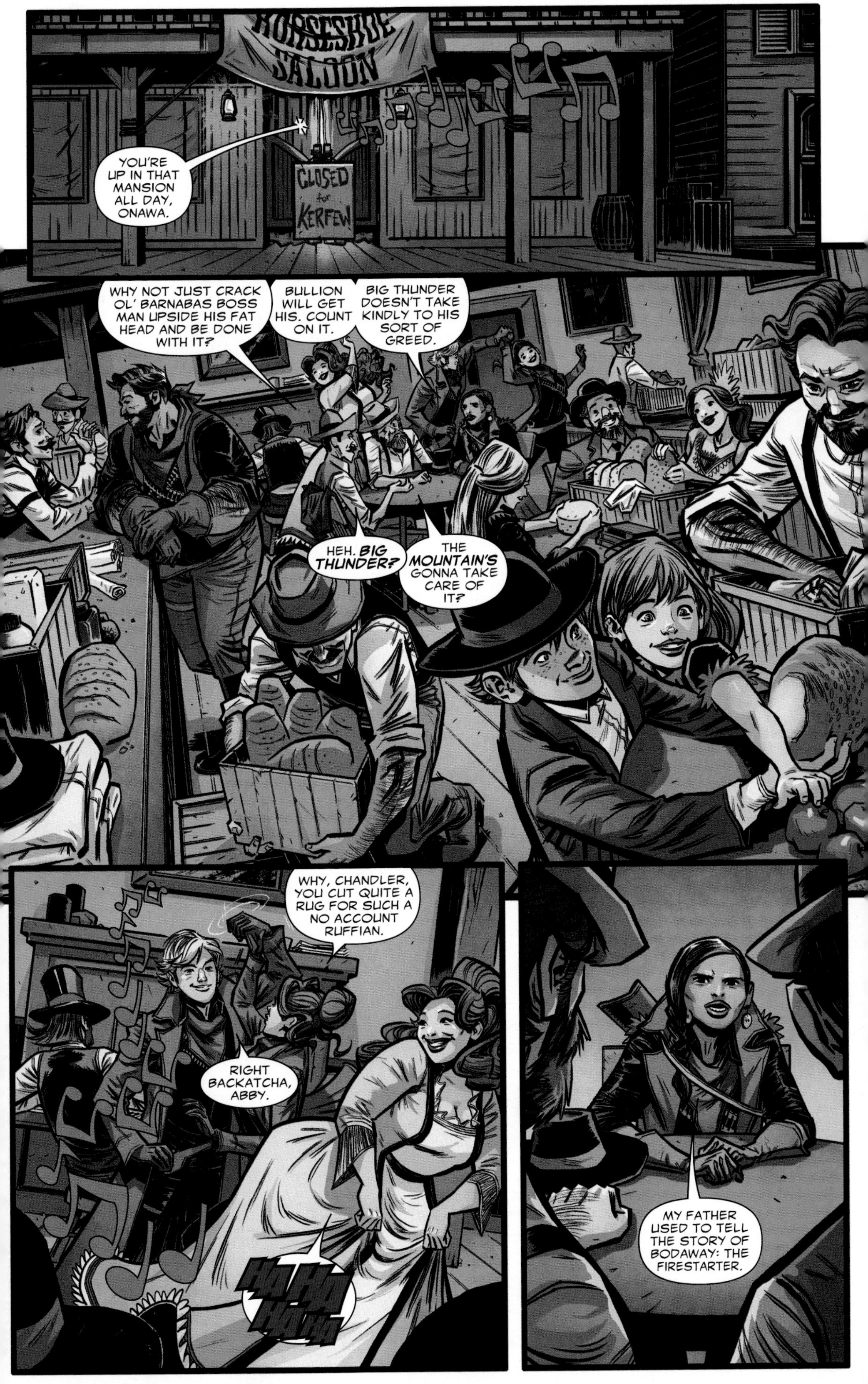
HORSESHOE SALOON
CLOSED for KERFEW
YOU'RE UP IN THAT MANSION ALL DAY, ONAWA.
WHY NOT JUST CRACK OL' BARNABAS BOSS MAN UPSIDE HIS FAT HEAD AND BE DONE WITH IT?
BULLION WILL GET HIS. COUNT ON IT.
BIG THUNDER DOESN'T TAKE KINDLY TO HIS SORT OF GREED.
HEH. **BIG THUNDER?**
THE **MOUNTAIN'S** GONNA TAKE CARE OF IT?
WHY, CHANDLER, YOU CUT QUITE A RUG FOR SUCH A NO ACCOUNT RUFFIAN.
RIGHT BACKATCHA, ABBY.
HA HA HA HA
MY FATHER USED TO TELL THE STORY OF BODAWAY: THE FIRESTARTER.

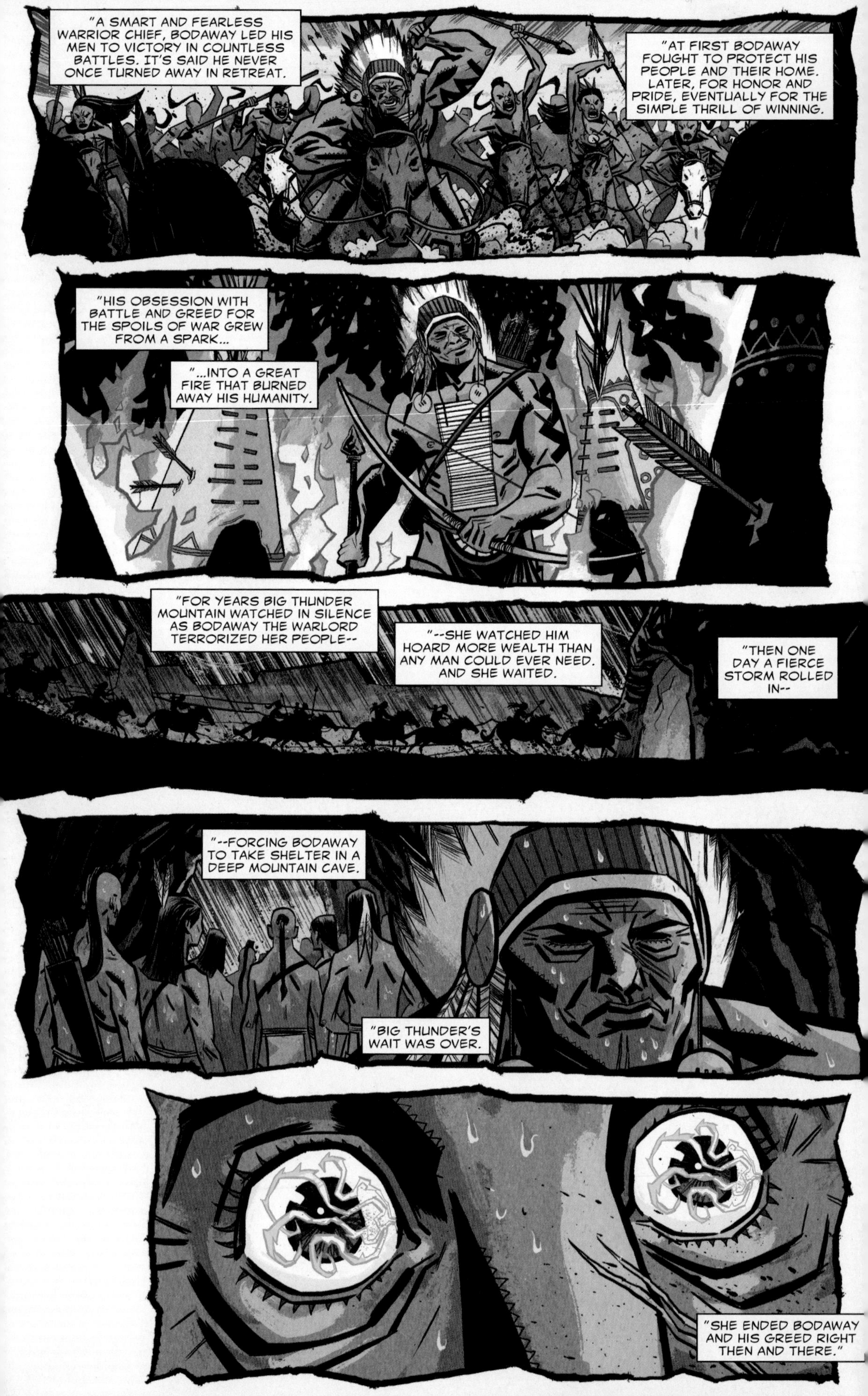
"A SMART AND FEARLESS WARRIOR CHIEF, BODAWAY LED HIS MEN TO VICTORY IN COUNTLESS BATTLES. IT'S SAID HE NEVER ONCE TURNED AWAY IN RETREAT.
"AT FIRST BODAWAY FOUGHT TO PROTECT HIS PEOPLE AND THEIR HOME. LATER, FOR HONOR AND PRIDE, EVENTUALLY FOR THE SIMPLE THRILL OF WINNING.
"HIS OBSESSION WITH BATTLE AND GREED FOR THE SPOILS OF WAR GREW FROM A SPARK...
"...INTO A GREAT FIRE THAT BURNED AWAY HIS HUMANITY.
"FOR YEARS BIG THUNDER MOUNTAIN WATCHED IN SILENCE AS BODAWAY THE WARLORD TERRORIZED HER PEOPLE--
"--SHE WATCHED HIM HOARD MORE WEALTH THAN ANY MAN COULD EVER NEED. AND SHE WAITED.
"THEN ONE DAY A FIERCE STORM ROLLED IN--
"--FORCING BODAWAY TO TAKE SHELTER IN A DEEP MOUNTAIN CAVE.
"BIG THUNDER'S WAIT WAS OVER.
"SHE ENDED BODAWAY AND HIS GREED RIGHT THEN AND THERE."

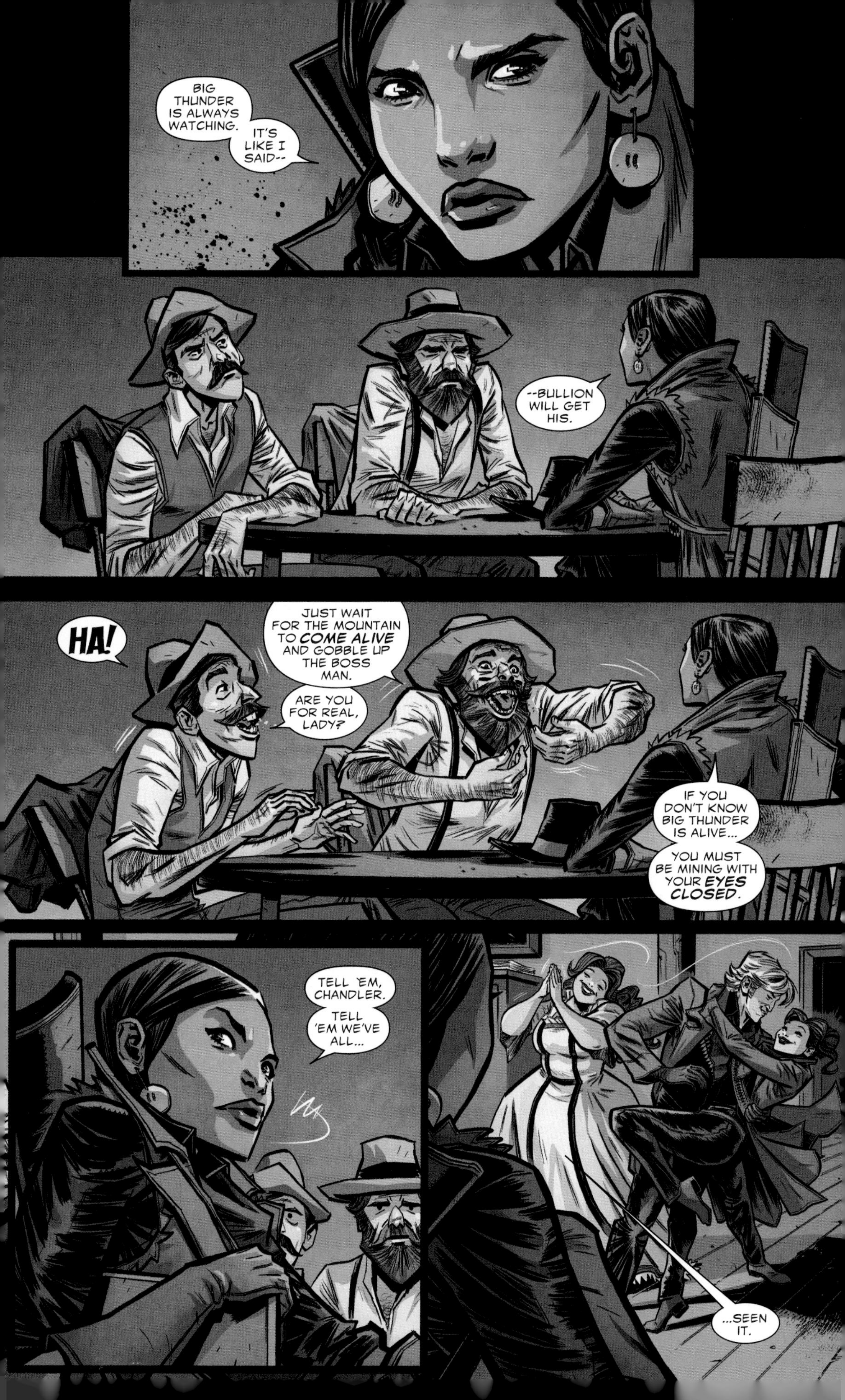
BIG THUNDER IS ALWAYS WATCHING.
IT'S LIKE I SAID--
--BULLION WILL GET HIS.
HA!
JUST WAIT FOR THE MOUNTAIN TO COME ALIVE AND GOBBLE UP THE BOSS MAN.
ARE YOU FOR REAL, LADY?
IF YOU DON'T KNOW BIG THUNDER IS ALIVE...
YOU MUST BE MINING WITH YOUR EYES CLOSED.
TELL 'EM, CHANDLER.
TELL 'EM WE'VE ALL...
...SEEN IT.

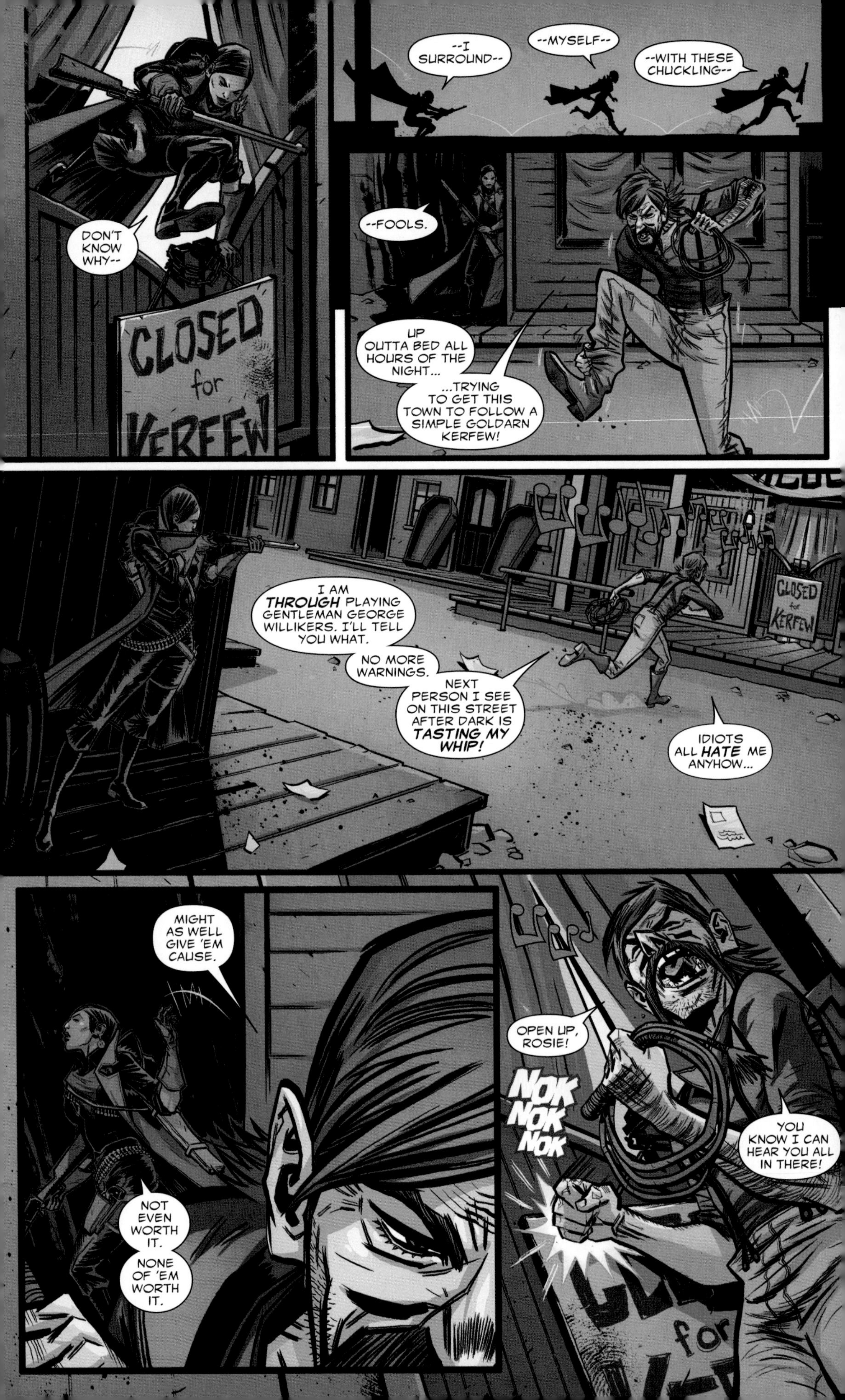
DON'T KNOW WHY--
CLOSED for KERFEW
--I SURROUND--
--MYSELF--
--WITH THESE CHUCKLING--
--FOOLS.
UP OUTTA BED ALL HOURS OF THE NIGHT...
...TRYING TO GET THIS TOWN TO FOLLOW A SIMPLE GOLDARN KERFEW!
I AM THROUGH PLAYING GENTLEMAN GEORGE WILLIKERS. I'LL TELL YOU WHAT.
NO MORE WARNINGS.
NEXT PERSON I SEE ON THIS STREET AFTER DARK IS TASTING MY WHIP!
CLOSED for KERFEW
IDIOTS ALL HATE ME ANYHOW...
MIGHT AS WELL GIVE 'EM CAUSE.
NOT EVEN WORTH IT.
NONE OF 'EM WORTH IT.
OPEN UP, ROSIE!
NOK NOK NOK
YOU KNOW I CAN HEAR YOU ALL IN THERE!

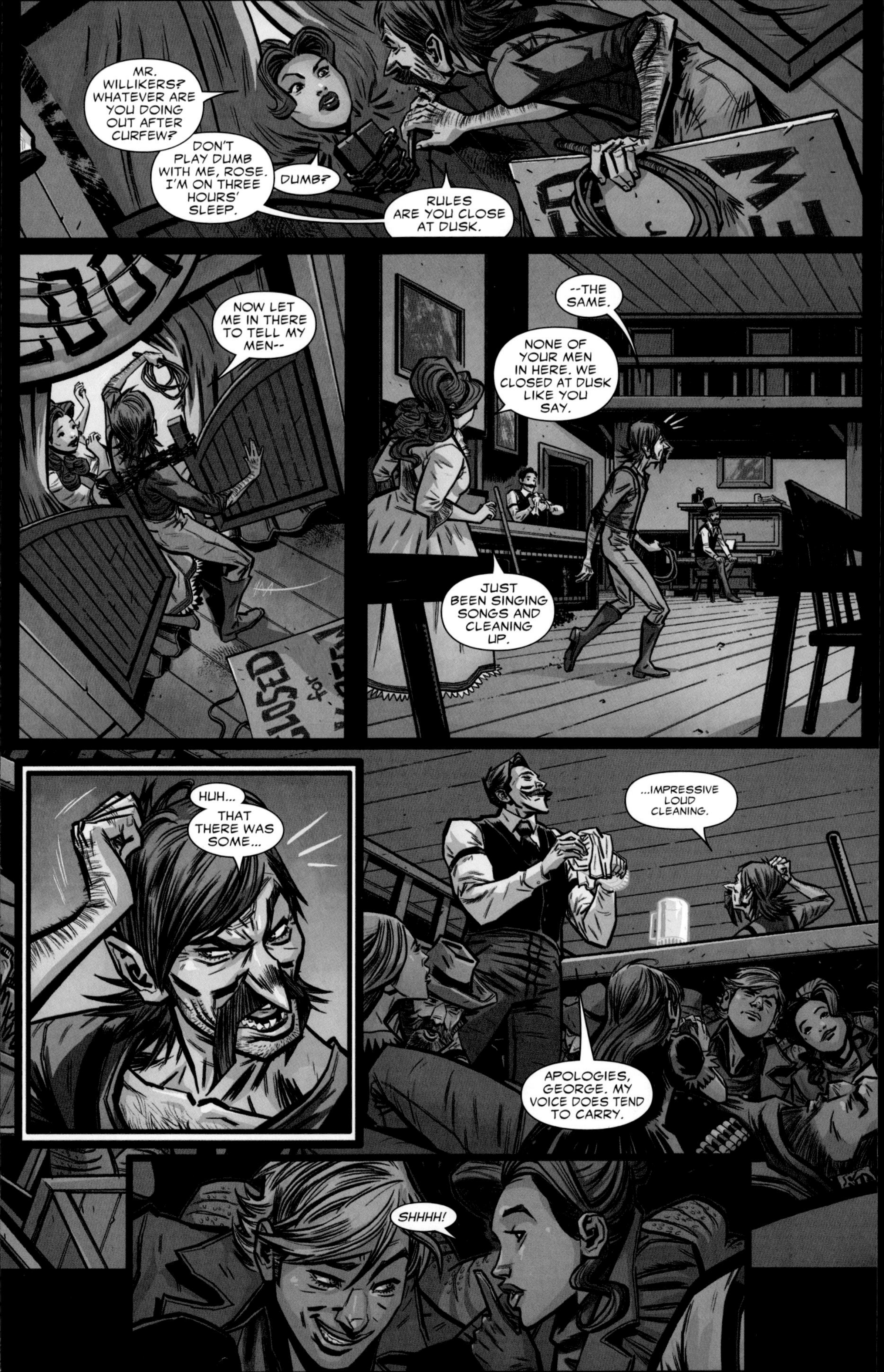
MR. WILLIKERS? WHATEVER ARE YOU DOING OUT AFTER CURFEW?
DON'T PLAY DUMB WITH ME, ROSE. I'M ON THREE HOURS' SLEEP.
DUMB?
RULES ARE YOU CLOSE AT DUSK.
NOW LET ME IN THERE TO TELL MY MEN--
--THE SAME.
NONE OF YOUR MEN IN HERE. WE CLOSED AT DUSK LIKE YOU SAY.
JUST BEEN SINGING SONGS AND CLEANING UP.
HUH... THAT THERE WAS SOME...
...IMPRESSIVE LOUD CLEANING.
APOLOGIES, GEORGE. MY VOICE DOES TEND TO CARRY.
SHHHH!

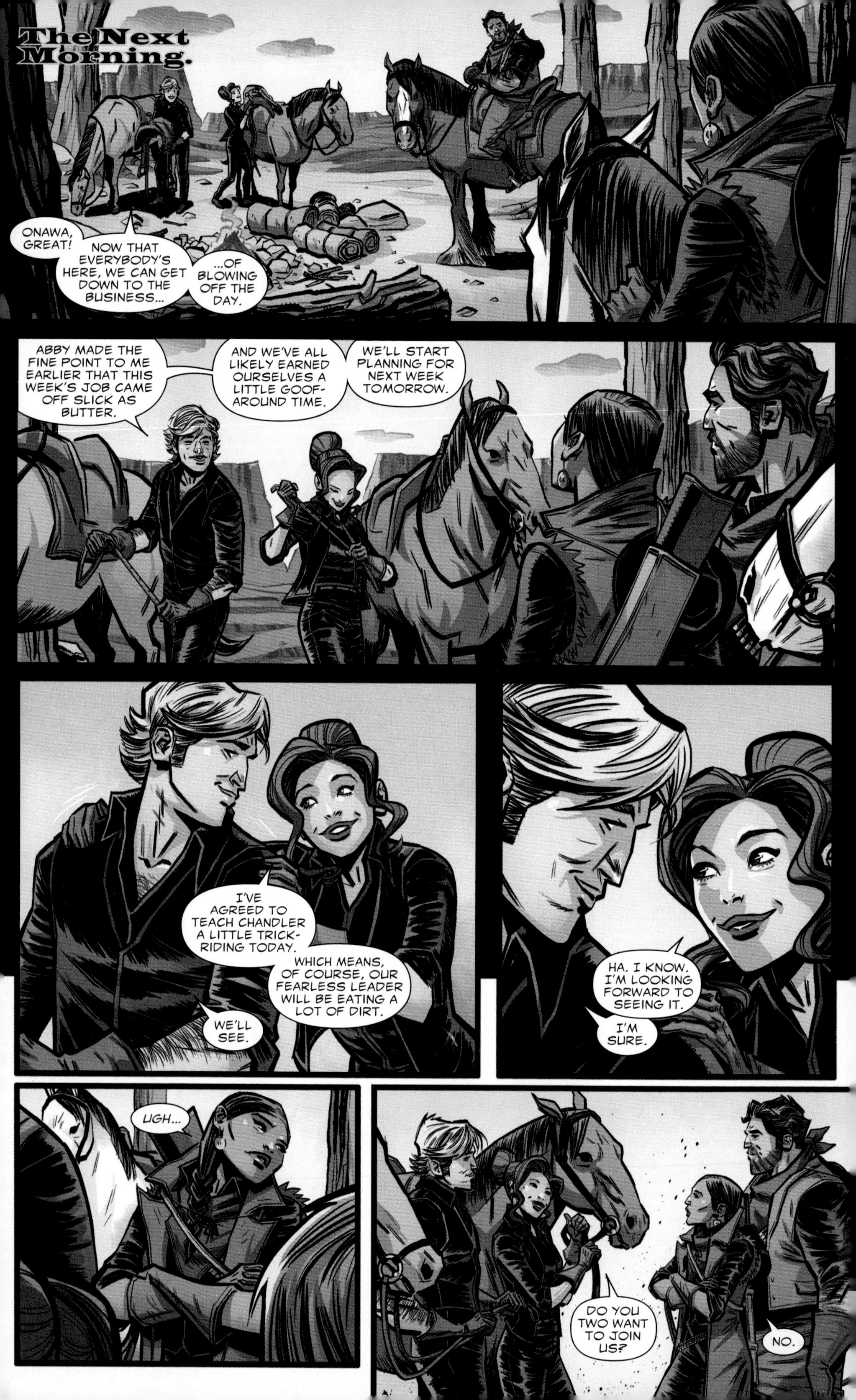
The Next Morning.
ONAWA, GREAT!
NOW THAT EVERYBODY'S HERE, WE CAN GET DOWN TO THE BUSINESS...
...OF BLOWING OFF THE DAY.
ABBY MADE THE FINE POINT TO ME EARLIER THAT THIS WEEK'S JOB CAME OFF SLICK AS BUTTER.
AND WE'VE ALL LIKELY EARNED OURSELVES A LITTLE GOOF-AROUND TIME.
WE'LL START PLANNING FOR NEXT WEEK TOMORROW.
I'VE AGREED TO TEACH CHANDLER A LITTLE TRICK-RIDING TODAY.
WHICH MEANS, OF COURSE, OUR FEARLESS LEADER WILL BE EATING A LOT OF DIRT.
WE'LL SEE.
HA. I KNOW. I'M LOOKING FORWARD TO SEEING IT.
I'M SURE.
UGH...
DO YOU TWO WANT TO JOIN US?
NO.

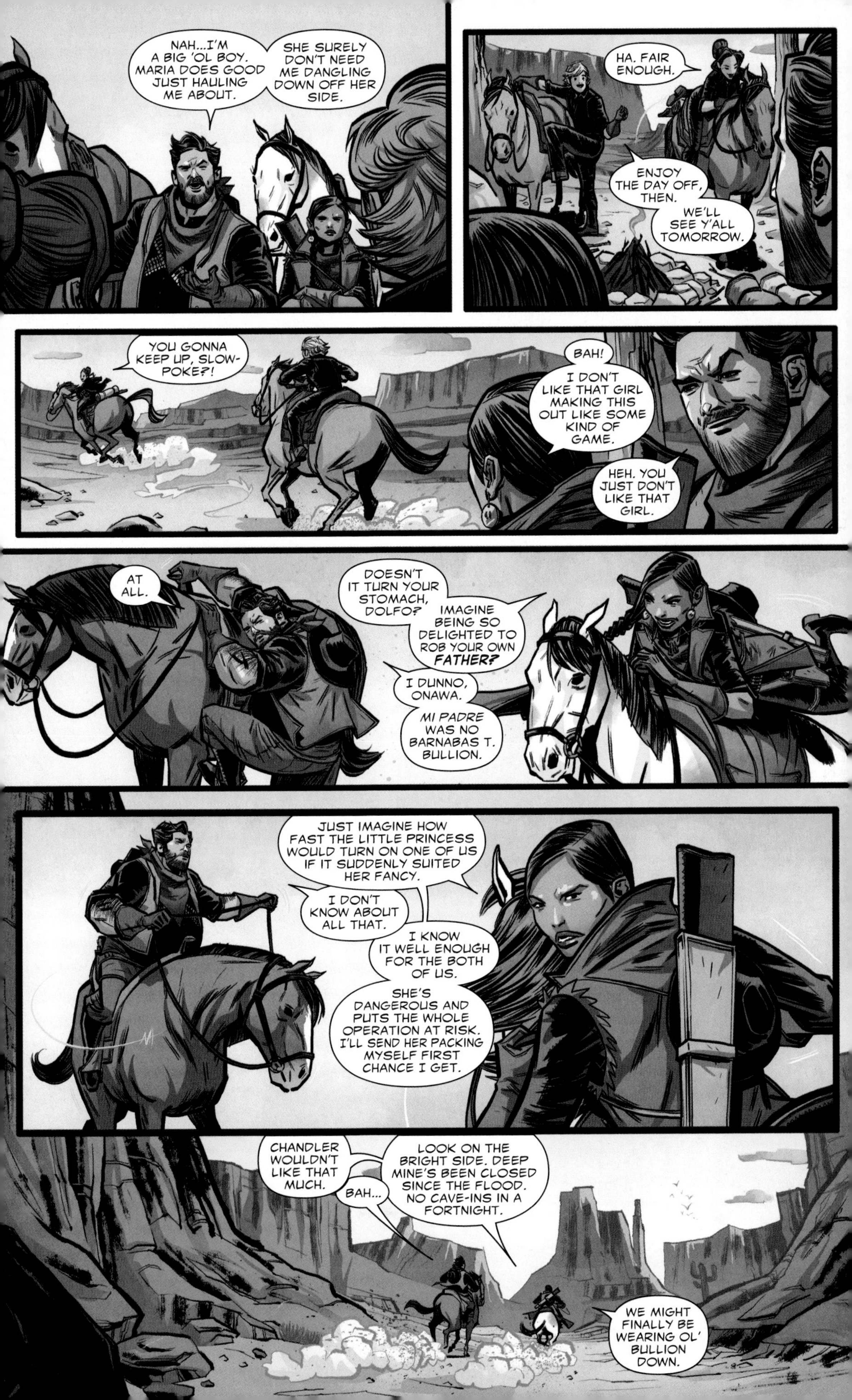
NAH...I'M A BIG 'OL BOY. MARIA DOES GOOD JUST HAULING ME ABOUT.
SHE SURELY DON'T NEED ME DANGLING DOWN OFF HER SIDE.
HA. FAIR ENOUGH.
ENJOY THE DAY OFF, THEN.
WE'LL SEE Y'ALL TOMORROW.
YOU GONNA KEEP UP, SLOW-POKE?!
BAH!
I DON'T LIKE THAT GIRL MAKING THIS OUT LIKE SOME KIND OF GAME.
HEH. YOU JUST DON'T LIKE THAT GIRL.
AT ALL.
DOESN'T IT TURN YOUR STOMACH, DOLFO?
IMAGINE BEING SO DELIGHTED TO ROB YOUR OWN *FATHER?*
I DUNNO, ONAWA.
*MI PADRE* WAS NO BARNABAS T. BULLION.
JUST IMAGINE HOW FAST THE LITTLE PRINCESS WOULD TURN ON ONE OF US IF IT SUDDENLY SUITED HER FANCY.
I DON'T KNOW ABOUT ALL THAT.
I KNOW IT WELL ENOUGH FOR THE BOTH OF US.
SHE'S DANGEROUS AND PUTS THE WHOLE OPERATION AT RISK. I'LL SEND HER PACKING MYSELF FIRST CHANCE I GET.
CHANDLER WOULDN'T LIKE THAT MUCH.
BAH...
LOOK ON THE BRIGHT SIDE. DEEP MINE'S BEEN CLOSED SINCE THE FLOOD. NO CAVE-INS IN A FORTNIGHT.
WE MIGHT FINALLY BE WEARING OL' BULLION DOWN.

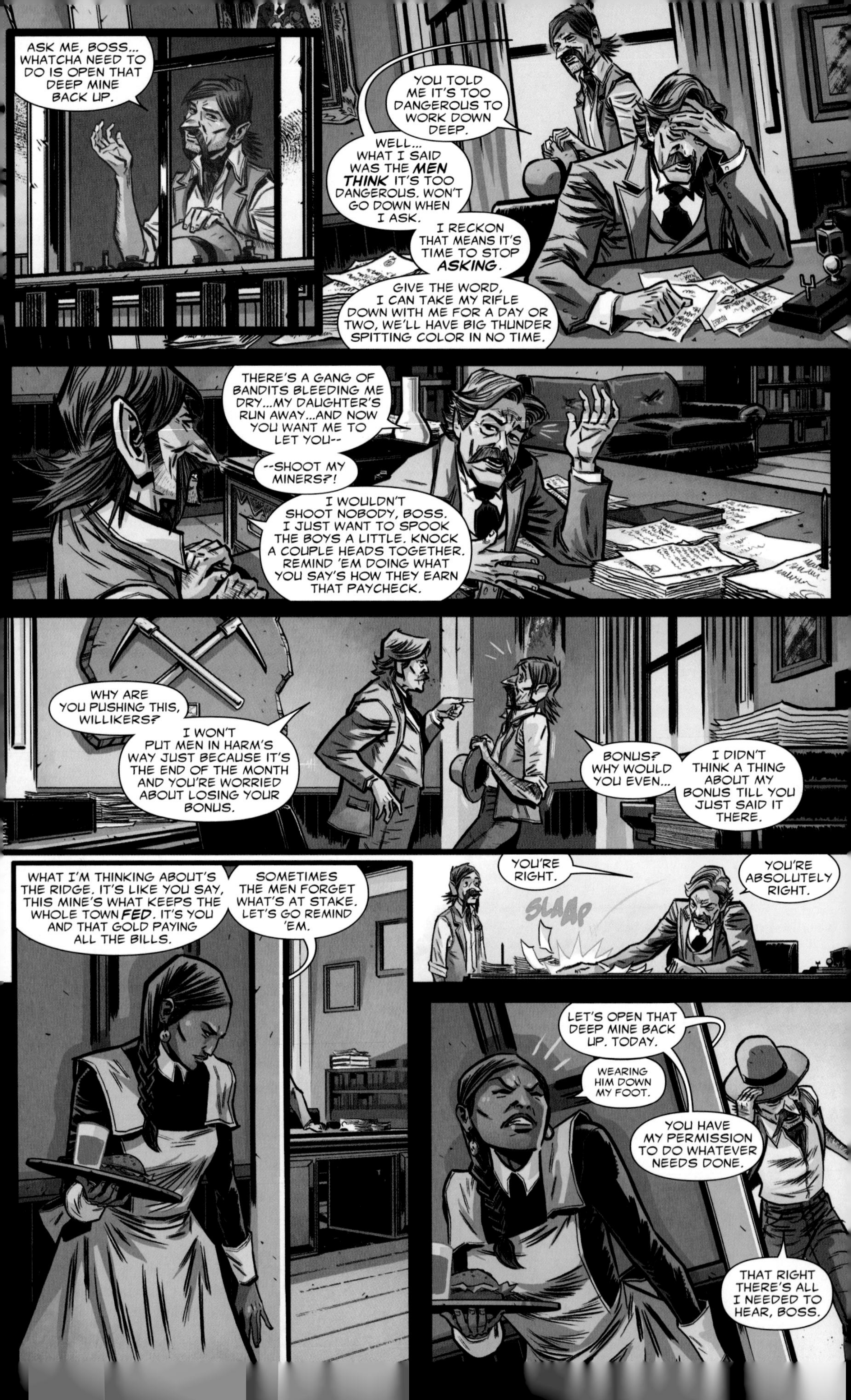
ASK ME, BOSS... WHATCHA NEED TO DO IS OPEN THAT DEEP MINE BACK UP.
YOU TOLD ME IT'S TOO DANGEROUS TO WORK DOWN DEEP.
WELL... WHAT I SAID WAS THE MEN THINK IT'S TOO DANGEROUS. WON'T GO DOWN WHEN I ASK.
I RECKON THAT MEANS IT'S TIME TO STOP ASKING.
GIVE THE WORD, I CAN TAKE MY RIFLE DOWN WITH ME FOR A DAY OR TWO, WE'LL HAVE BIG THUNDER SPITTING COLOR IN NO TIME.
THERE'S A GANG OF BANDITS BLEEDING ME DRY...MY DAUGHTER'S RUN AWAY...AND NOW YOU WANT ME TO LET YOU--
--SHOOT MY MINERS?!
I WOULDN'T SHOOT NOBODY, BOSS. I JUST WANT TO SPOOK THE BOYS A LITTLE. KNOCK A COUPLE HEADS TOGETHER. REMIND 'EM DOING WHAT YOU SAY'S HOW THEY EARN THAT PAYCHECK.
WHY ARE YOU PUSHING THIS, WILLIKERS?
I WON'T PUT MEN IN HARM'S WAY JUST BECAUSE IT'S THE END OF THE MONTH AND YOU'RE WORRIED ABOUT LOSING YOUR BONUS.
BONUS? WHY WOULD YOU EVEN...
I DIDN'T THINK A THING ABOUT MY BONUS TILL YOU JUST SAID IT THERE.
WHAT I'M THINKING ABOUT'S THE RIDGE. IT'S LIKE YOU SAY, THIS MINE'S WHAT KEEPS THE WHOLE TOWN FED. IT'S YOU AND THAT GOLD PAYING ALL THE BILLS.
SOMETIMES THE MEN FORGET WHAT'S AT STAKE. LET'S GO REMIND 'EM.
YOU'RE RIGHT.
SLAAP
YOU'RE ABSOLUTELY RIGHT.
LET'S OPEN THAT DEEP MINE BACK UP. TODAY.
WEARING HIM DOWN MY FOOT.
YOU HAVE MY PERMISSION TO DO WHATEVER NEEDS DONE.
THAT RIGHT THERE'S ALL I NEEDED TO HEAR, BOSS.

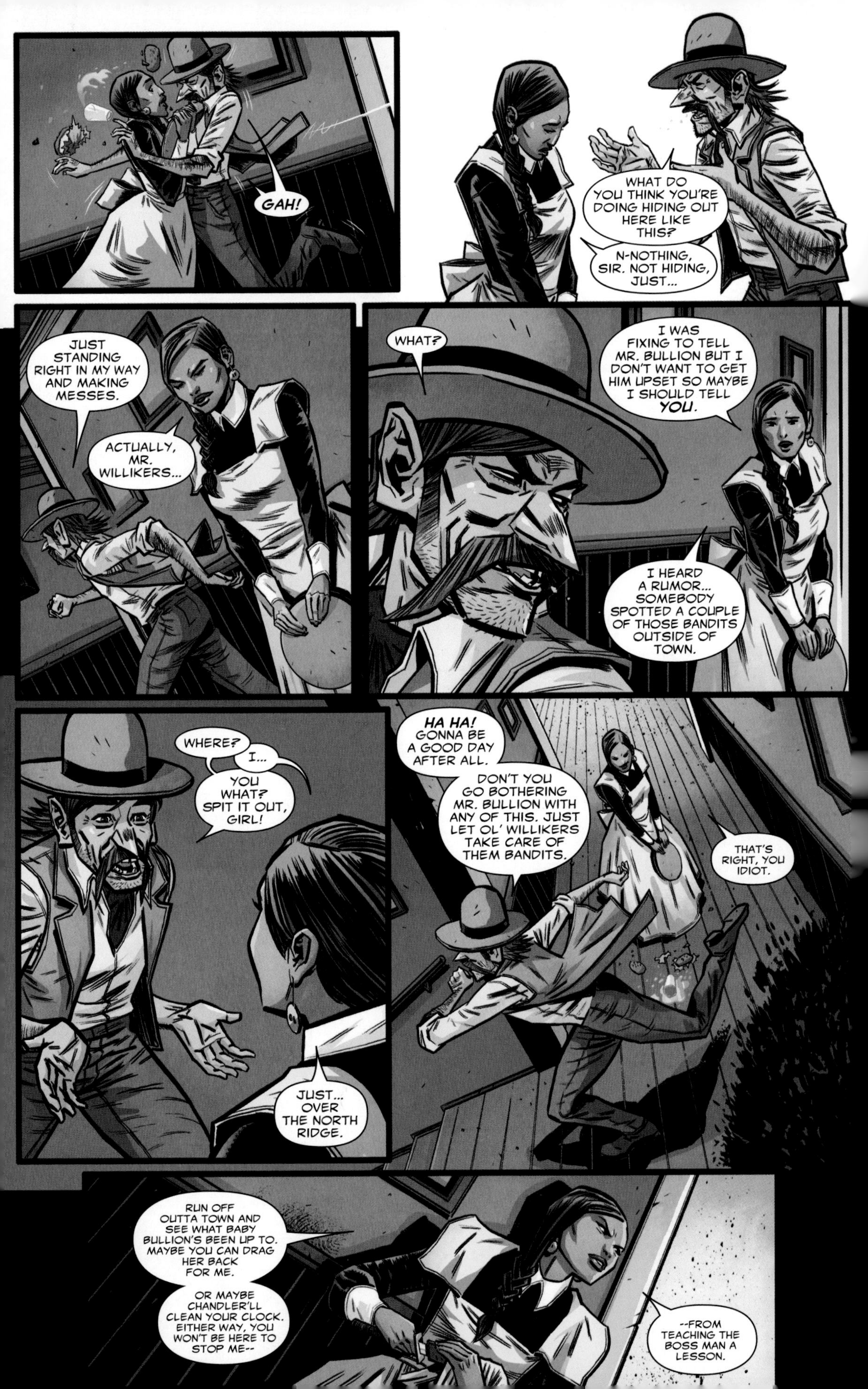
GAH!
WHAT DO YOU THINK YOU'RE DOING HIDING OUT HERE LIKE THIS?
N-NOTHING, SIR. NOT HIDING, JUST...
JUST STANDING RIGHT IN MY WAY AND MAKING MESSES.
ACTUALLY, MR. WILLIKERS...
WHAT?
I WAS FIXING TO TELL MR. BULLION BUT I DON'T WANT TO GET HIM UPSET SO MAYBE I SHOULD TELL YOU.
I HEARD A RUMOR... SOMEBODY SPOTTED A COUPLE OF THOSE BANDITS OUTSIDE OF TOWN.
WHERE?
I...
YOU WHAT? SPIT IT OUT, GIRL!
JUST... OVER THE NORTH RIDGE.
HA HA! GONNA BE A GOOD DAY AFTER ALL.
DON'T YOU GO BOTHERING MR. BULLION WITH ANY OF THIS. JUST LET OL' WILLIKERS TAKE CARE OF THEM BANDITS.
THAT'S RIGHT, YOU IDIOT.
RUN OFF OUTTA TOWN AND SEE WHAT BABY BULLION'S BEEN UP TO. MAYBE YOU CAN DRAG HER BACK FOR ME.
OR MAYBE CHANDLER'LL CLEAN YOUR CLOCK. EITHER WAY, YOU WON'T BE HERE TO STOP ME--
--FROM TEACHING THE BOSS MAN A LESSON.

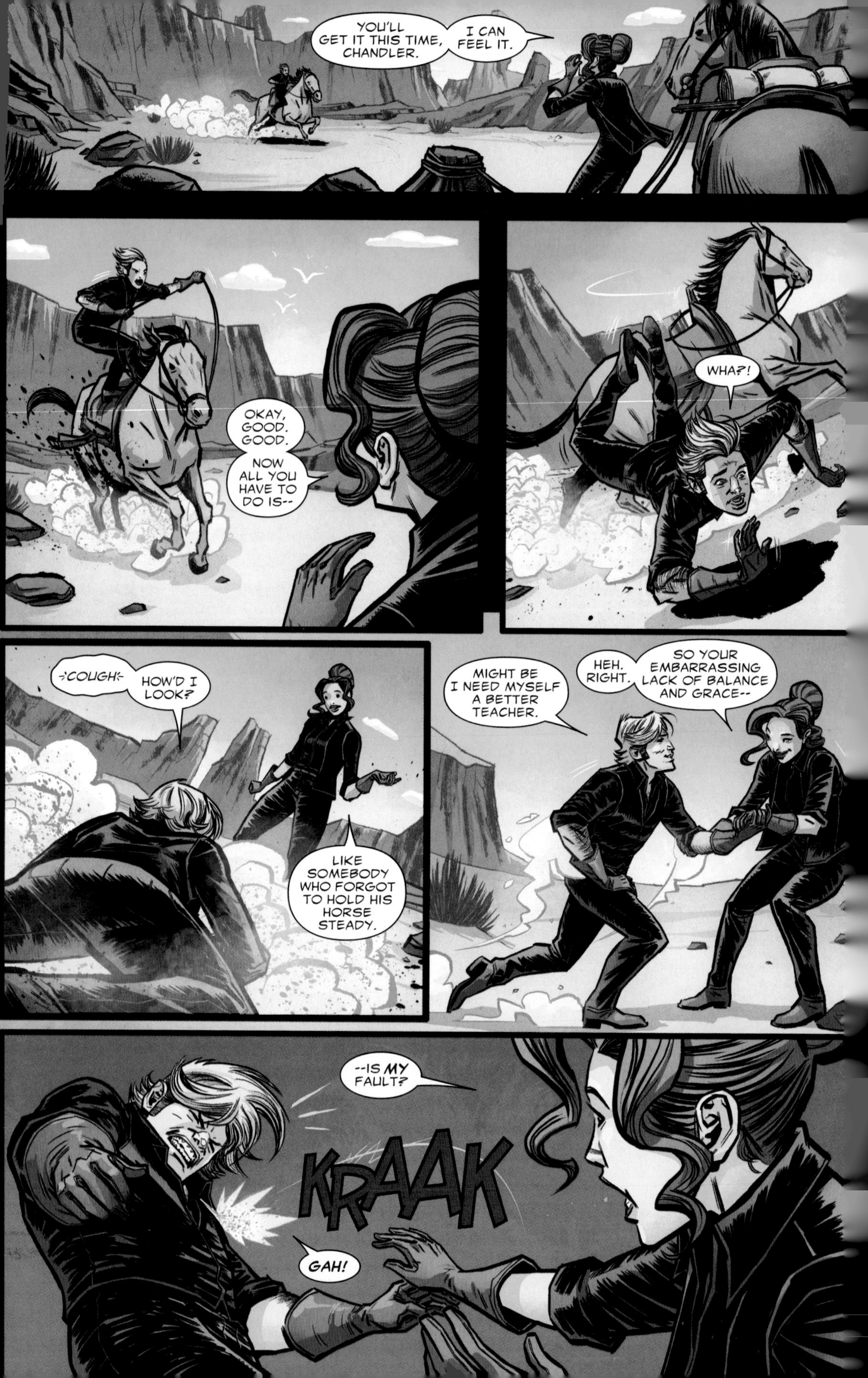
YOU'LL GET IT THIS TIME, CHANDLER.
I CAN FEEL IT.
OKAY, GOOD. GOOD.
NOW ALL YOU HAVE TO DO IS--
WHA?!
-COUGH-
HOW'D I LOOK?
LIKE SOMEBODY WHO FORGOT TO HOLD HIS HORSE STEADY.
MIGHT BE I NEED MYSELF A BETTER TEACHER.
HEH. RIGHT.
SO YOUR EMBARRASSING LACK OF BALANCE AND GRACE--
--IS MY FAULT?
KRAAK
GAH!

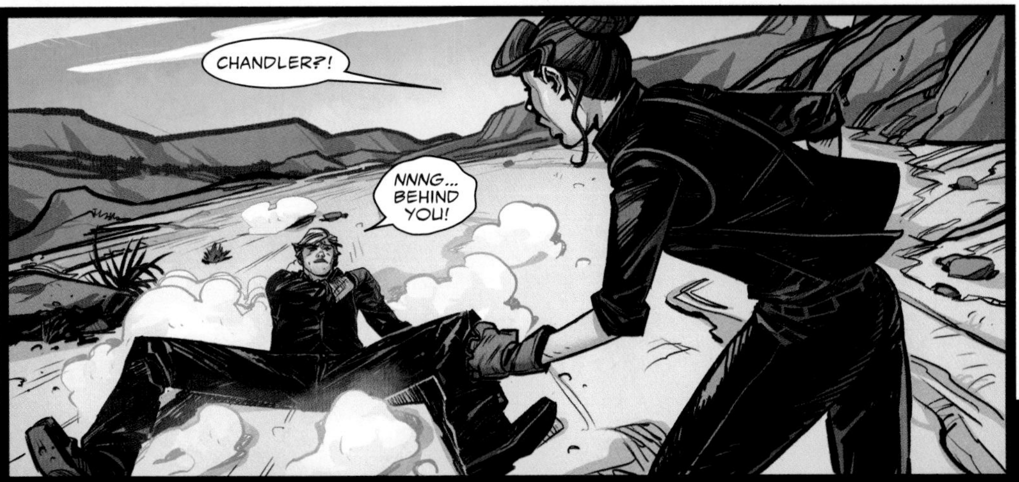
CHANDLER?!
NNNG... BEHIND YOU!

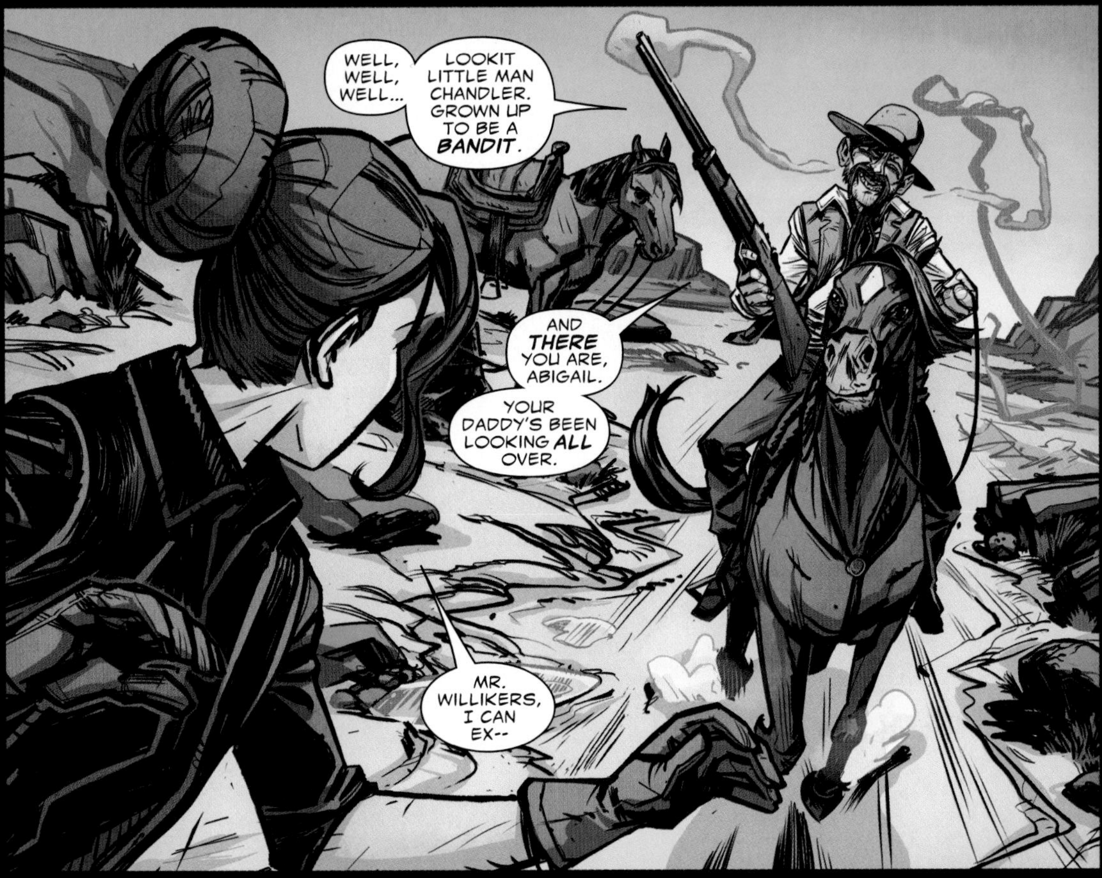
WELL, WELL, WELL...
LOOKIT LITTLE MAN CHANDLER. GROWN UP TO BE A BANDIT.
AND THERE YOU ARE, ABIGAIL.
YOUR DADDY'S BEEN LOOKING ALL OVER.
MR. WILLIKERS, I CAN EX--

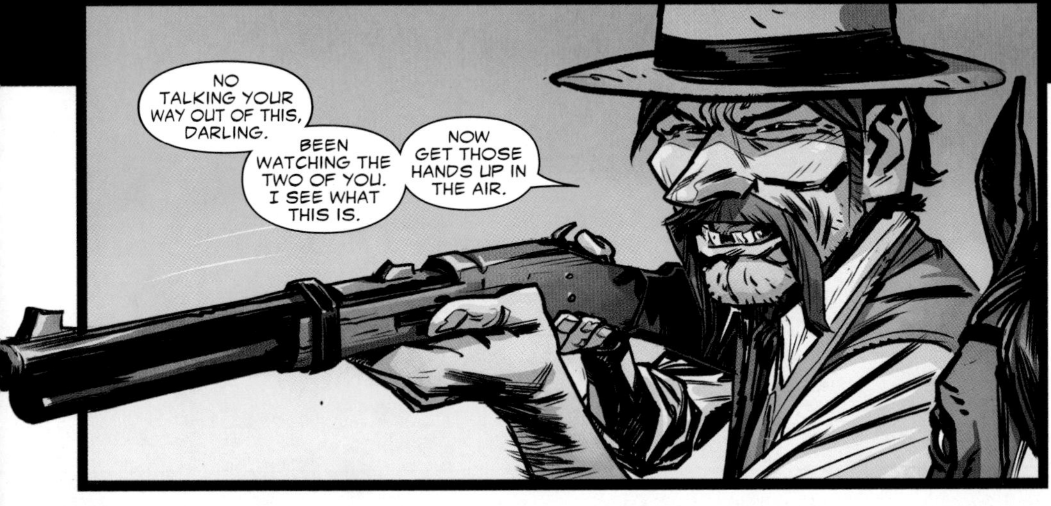
NO TALKING YOUR WAY OUT OF THIS, DARLING.
BEEN WATCHING THE TWO OF YOU. I SEE WHAT THIS IS.
NOW GET THOSE HANDS UP IN THE AIR.

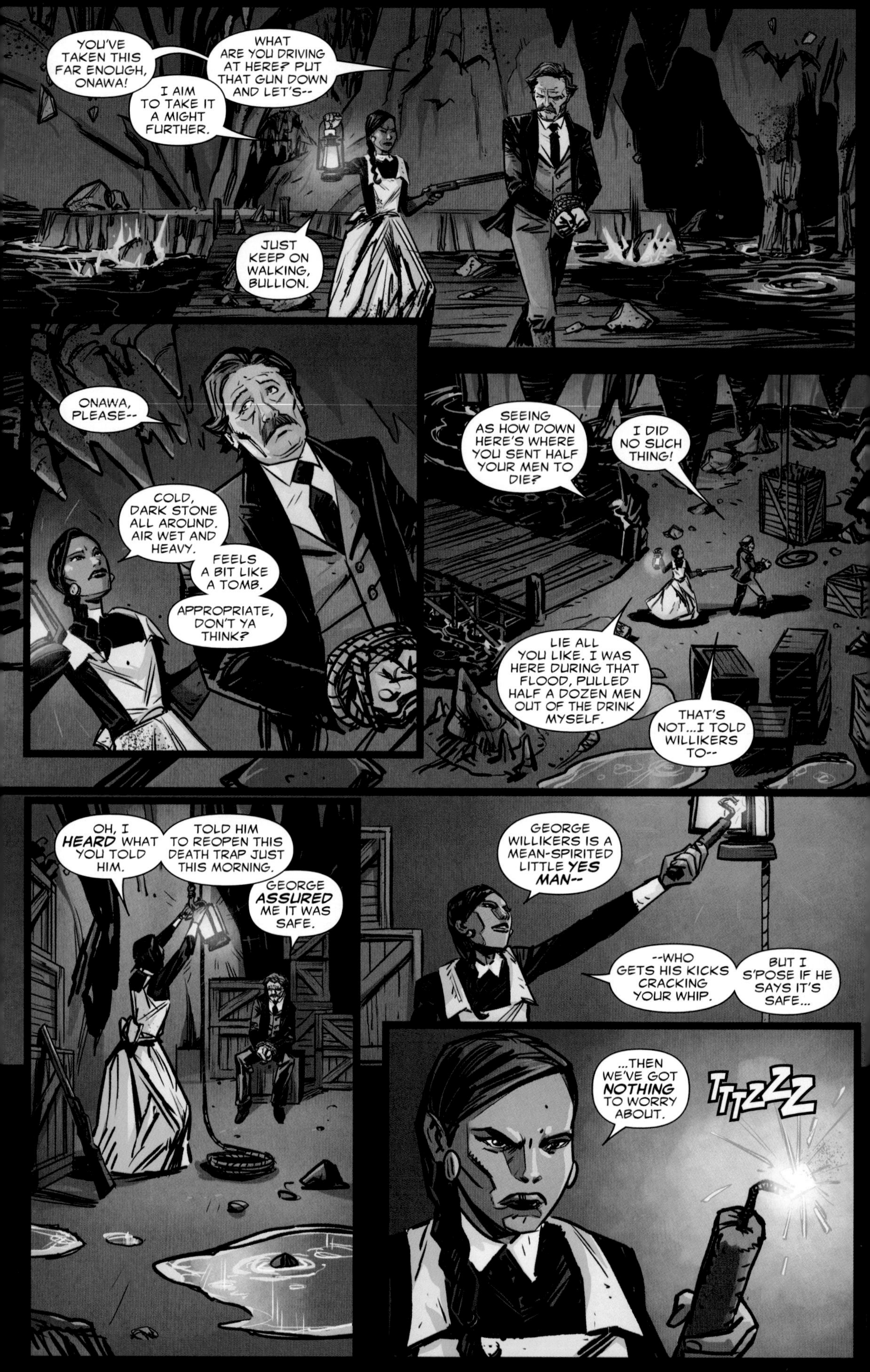
YOU'VE TAKEN THIS FAR ENOUGH, ONAWA!
WHAT ARE YOU DRIVING AT HERE? PUT THAT GUN DOWN AND LET'S--
I AIM TO TAKE IT A MIGHT FURTHER.
JUST KEEP ON WALKING, BULLION.
ONAWA, PLEASE--
COLD, DARK STONE ALL AROUND. AIR WET AND HEAVY.
FEELS A BIT LIKE A TOMB.
APPROPRIATE, DON'T YA THINK?
SEEING AS HOW DOWN HERE'S WHERE YOU SENT HALF YOUR MEN TO DIE?
I DID NO SUCH THING!
LIE ALL YOU LIKE. I WAS HERE DURING THAT FLOOD, PULLED HALF A DOZEN MEN OUT OF THE DRINK MYSELF.
THAT'S NOT...I TOLD WILLIKERS TO--
OH, I HEARD WHAT YOU TOLD HIM.
TOLD HIM TO REOPEN THIS DEATH TRAP JUST THIS MORNING.
GEORGE ASSURED ME IT WAS SAFE.
GEORGE WILLIKERS IS A MEAN-SPIRITED LITTLE YES MAN--
--WHO GETS HIS KICKS CRACKING YOUR WHIP.
BUT I S'POSE IF HE SAYS IT'S SAFE...
...THEN WE'VE GOT NOTHING TO WORRY ABOUT.
TTTZZZ

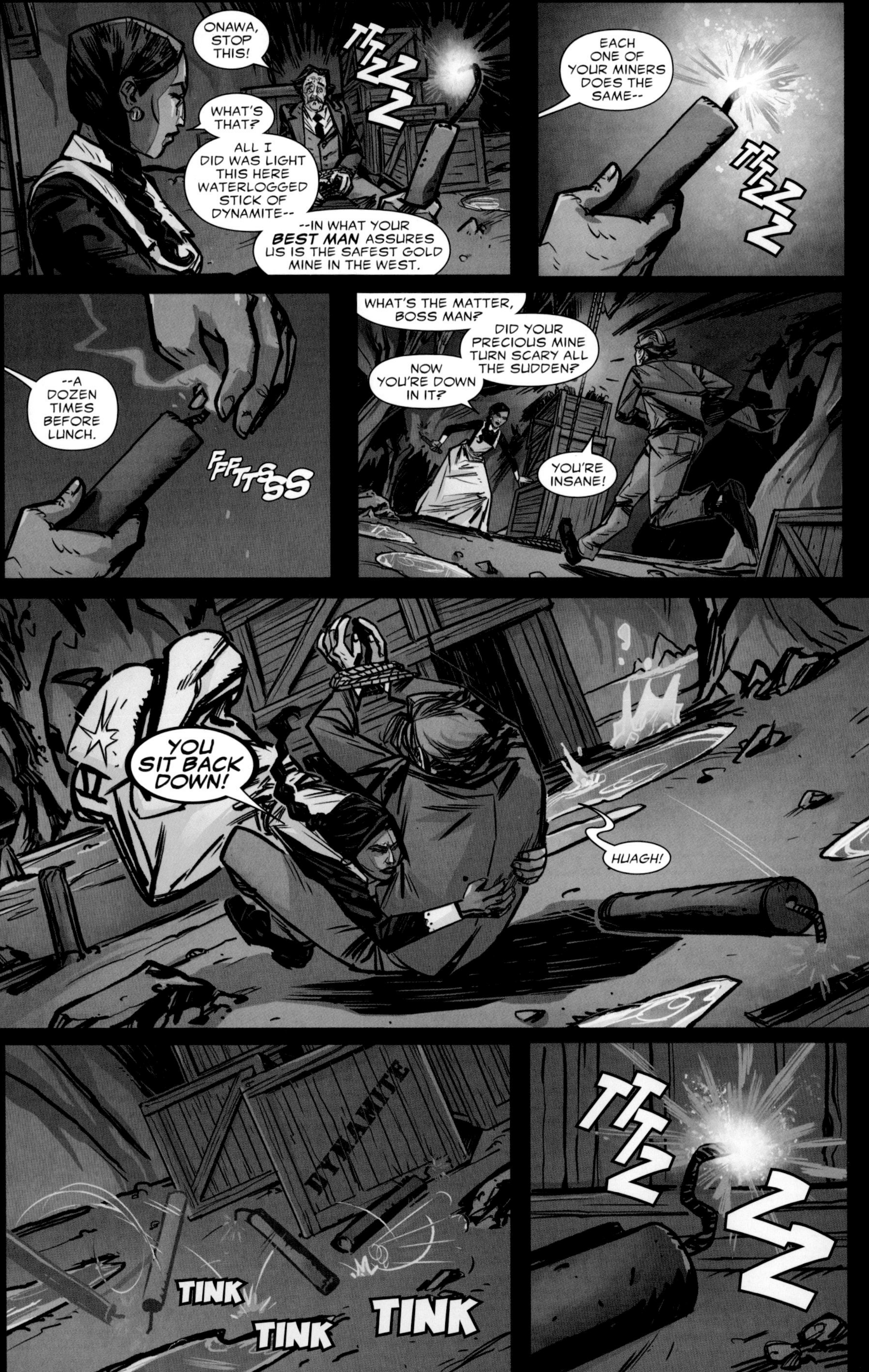
ONAWA, STOP THIS!
TTTZZZ
WHAT'S THAT?
ALL I DID WAS LIGHT THIS HERE WATERLOGGED STICK OF DYNAMITE--
--IN WHAT YOUR BEST MAN ASSURES US IS THE SAFEST GOLD MINE IN THE WEST.
EACH ONE OF YOUR MINERS DOES THE SAME--
TTTZZZ
--A DOZEN TIMES BEFORE LUNCH.
FFFTTSSSS
WHAT'S THE MATTER, BOSS MAN?
DID YOUR PRECIOUS MINE TURN SCARY ALL THE SUDDEN?
NOW YOU'RE DOWN IN IT?
YOU'RE INSANE!
YOU SIT BACK DOWN!
HUAGH!
DYNAMITE
TINK
TINK
TINK
TTTZZZ

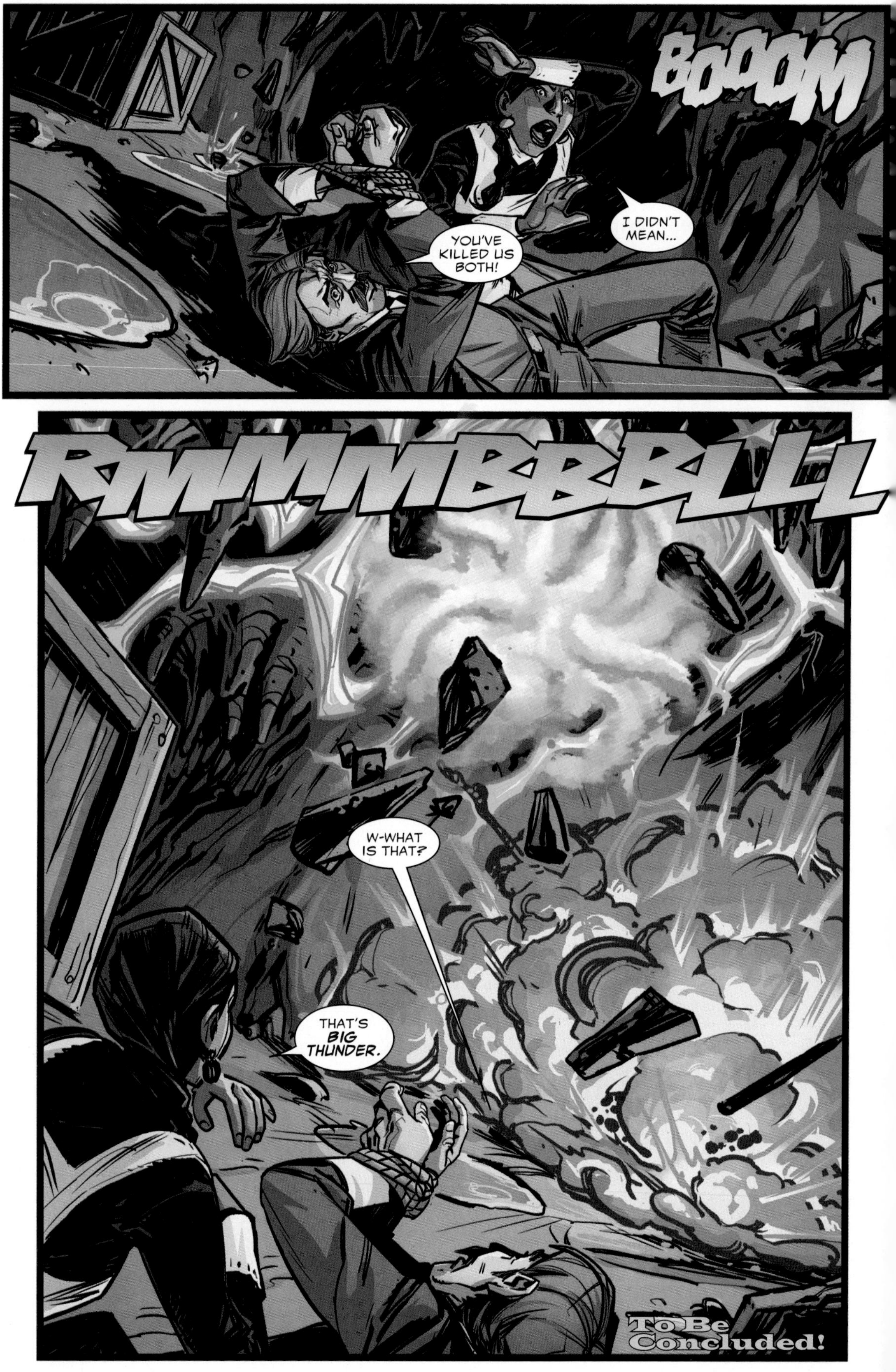
BOOOM
YOU'VE KILLED US BOTH!
I DIDN'T MEAN...
RMMMBBBLLL
W-WHAT IS THAT?
THAT'S BIG THUNDER.
To Be Concluded!

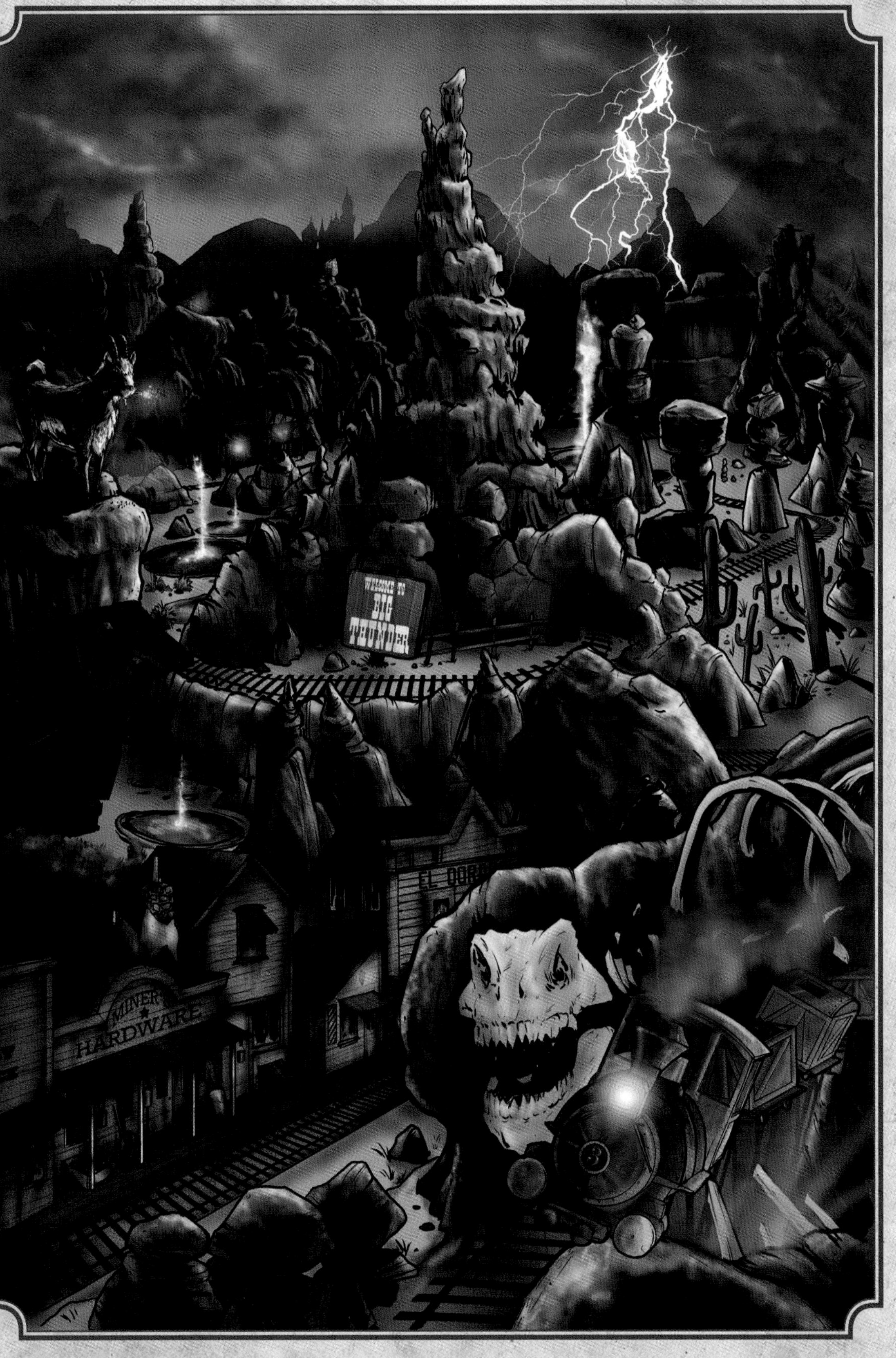
WELCOME TO
BIG
THUNDER
MINER'S
HARDWARE

***Big Thunder Mountain Railroad #1–4***
Connecting Variant Covers by Brian Crosby

Disney KINGDOMS

# BIG THUNDER MOUNTAIN RAILROAD

Disney KINGDOMS
BIG THUNDER
MOUNTAIN RAILROAD
#1
MARVEL
HOPELESS
WALKER
BEAULIEU

Hardcover Book ISBN
978-1-61479-575-9

## COLLECT THEM ALL!

**Set of 5**

**Hardcover Books ISBN:**
**978-1-61479-574-2**

Disney KINGDOMS
BIG THUNDER
MOUNTAIN RAILROAD
#2
MARVEL
HOPELESS
WALKER
BEAULIEU

Hardcover Book ISBN
978-1-61479-576-6

Disney KINGDOMS
BIG THUNDER
MOUNTAIN RAILROAD
#3
MARVEL
HOPELESS

Hardcover Book ISBN
978-1-61479-577-3

Disney KINGDOMS
BIG THUNDER
MOUNTAIN RAILROAD
#4
MARVEL
HOPELESS
WALKER
BEAULIEU

Hardcover Book ISBN
978-1-61479-578-0

Disney KINGDOMS
BIG THUNDER
MOUNTAIN RAILROAD
#5
MARVEL
HOPELESS
WALKER
MOGORRON
BEAULIEU

Hardcover Book ISBN
978-1-61479-579-7

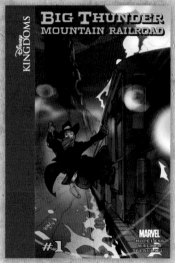

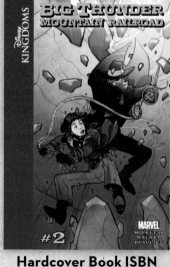

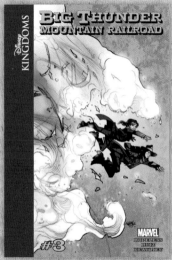

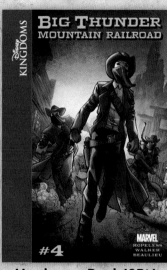

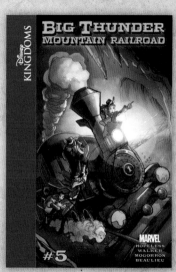